MEL BAY's

THE BUGLER'S HANDBOOK

By Nelson Knode

1 2 3 4 5 6 7 8 9 0

CONTENTS

BASICS OF BUGLE PLAYING

The regulation bugle in   G   is the most commonly used. Below is shown a small section of the piano keyboard. On the piano, play the four notes that are lettered.

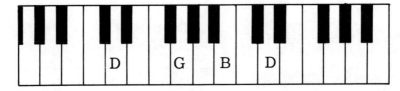

These four notes are all that is required of the average bugler. However the extended range will be very helpful for more elaborate calls and fanfares.

Posture is important, so stand straight and grasp the bugle lightly with the right hand as shown.

HOW TO PRODUCE A TONE

First place the mouthpiece on your lips about one third on the upper lip and about two thirds on the lower lip and in the center of the mouth.

With a slight smile, tongue the note as if you were pronouncing tee or tu and following it with a steady flow of air.

By doing the above one should be able to produce a sound that can be cultivated into a very fine tone.

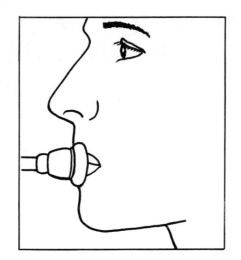

EXAMPLE OF LOCATION OF MOUTHPIECE ON LIPS

Now that you have produced a tone, try to match it with the four sounds on the piano.

If you don't have a piano, try to make four different pitches. Starting with the lowest and working each note up a little higher.

ACTUAL PITCH AND EXTENDED RANGE OF THE BUGLE IN -G-

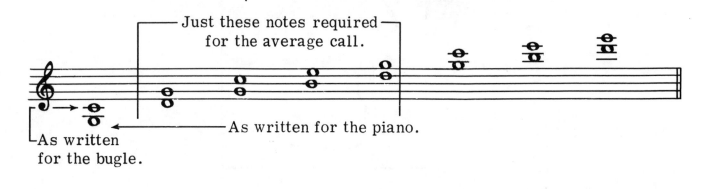

Just these notes required
for the average call.

As written for the piano.

As written
for the bugle.

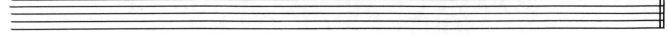

The five lines shown above are called a music staff.

This sign is called a - G - clef or <u>treble</u> clef.

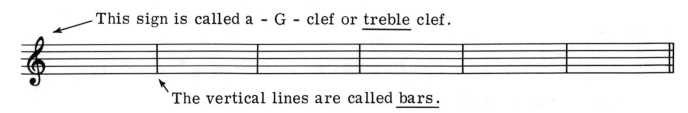

The vertical lines are called <u>bars</u>.

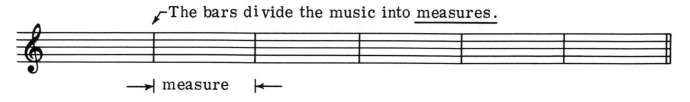

The bars divide the music into <u>measures</u>.

→| measure |←

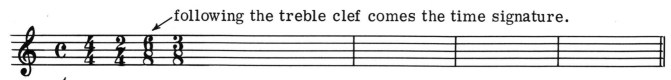

following the treble clef comes the time signature.

Five of the most common used time signatures are shown above.

C - Standing for common time or 4/4 time. Meaning there are four beats to the measure.

2/4 - Means there are two beats to a measure.

6/8 - Means there are six beats to a measure.

3/8 - Means there are three beats to a measure.

It is best to think of the top number as the number of beats in a measure. The bottom number is the type of note which would receive one beat.

WHOLE NOTE STUDY

Whole note $\circ$ = four beats sustained tone.

Whole rest ➖ = four beats of silence.

Double dot & double bar means repeat back to the beginning.

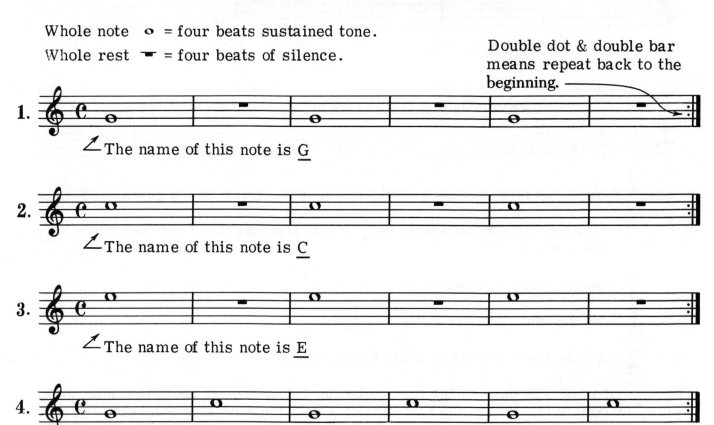

1. The name of this note is <u>G</u>

2. The name of this note is <u>C</u>

3. The name of this note is <u>E</u>

4.

CLIMB THE MOUNTAIN AND HOLD ON

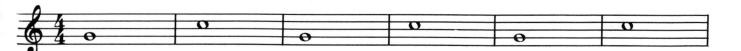

The name of this note is high G

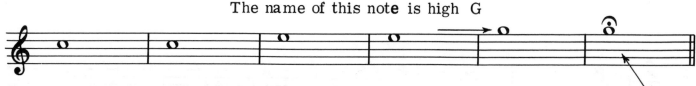

This is a hold sign, which means to hold the note as long as you wish.

HALF NOTE STUDY

♩ Half note = 2 beats.

━ Half rest = 2 beats of silence

1.

2.

3.

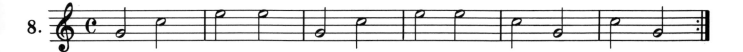

COME TO CHURCH
(A CALL)

Moderately

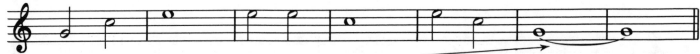

Tie both whole notes together
as one long note for the count of
eight beats.

WHOLE NOTE AND HALF NOTE STUDY

WASH UP
(A CALL)

Moderate

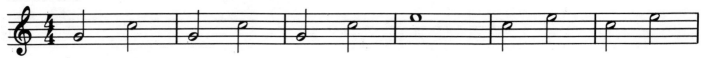

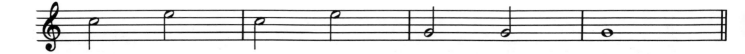

TIME TO PLAY

Moderate

QUARTER NOTE STUDY

AROUND ABOUT
(A CALL)

Fast

$\frac{3}{4}$ = 3 beats to the measure.

* ▬ Half rest = two beats of silence

WHERE DID YOU GET THAT DRUMMER

SLEEPY TIME

STUDY IN QUARTER NOTES,
HALF NOTES AND WHOLE NOTES.

3.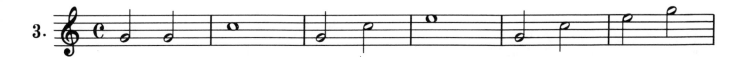

4.

LET'S GO TO SCHOOL

Moderate

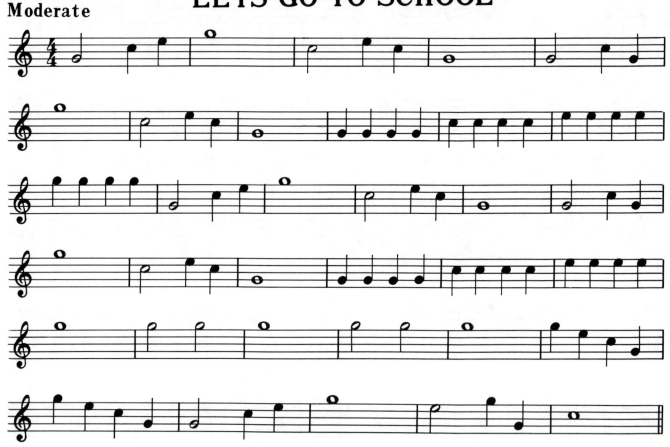

FAST DRILL

STUDY IN QUARTER NOTES AND RESTS
STUDY IN HALF NOTES AND RESTS
STUDY IN WHOLE NOTES AND RESTS

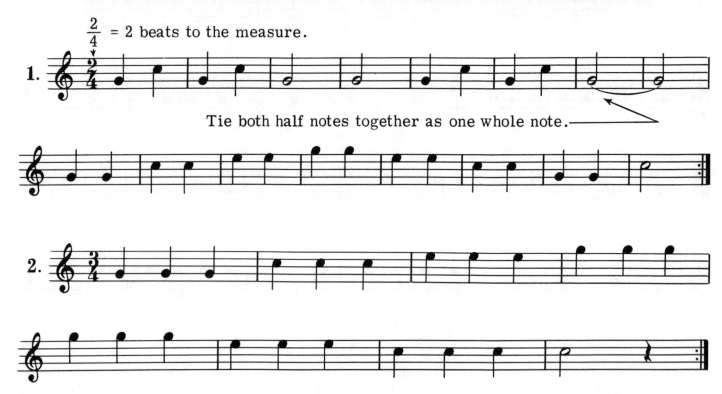

$\frac{2}{4}$ = 2 beats to the measure.

Tie both half notes together as one whole note.

3.

4.

STUDY IN EIGHTH NOTES, QUARTER NOTES, HALF NOTES AND WHOLE NOTES.

There are two eighth notes to one beat.

♪ = Eighth note.

♪♪♪♪ a group of eighth notes.

♪ = eighth rest - there are two eighth rests to one beat.

STUDY IN

Eighth notes and eighth rest.

Quarter notes and eighth rest.

Half notes and eighth rest.

Whole notes and eighth rest.

The following three pages are devoted to the most commonly used bugle calls.
They have been simplified so as not to be above the level of the student at this time.

TAPS

Full tone

MESS CALL

ASSEMBLY

Fast

FIRST CALL

Fast

REVEILLE

OLD TIMER

SIXTEENTH NOTE STUDY

♪ one sixteenth note = one quarter of a beat.

There are four sixteenth notes (♪♪♪♪) to a beat.

There are two sixteenth notes (♫) to one half a beat.

♪ one sixteenth rest = one quarter of a beat. (4 sixteenth rests= /quarter rest)

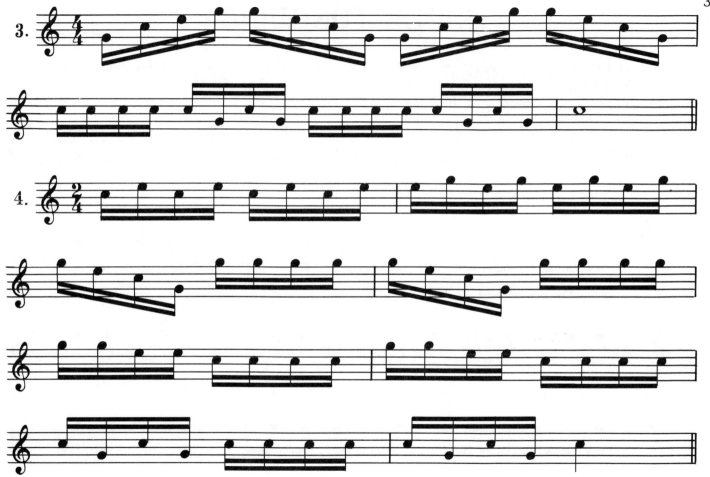

TRIPLE TONGUING

At this time it is very important to pay strict attention to triple tonguing.
The following studies are to be practiced slowly at first and as one progresses the speed may be increased.

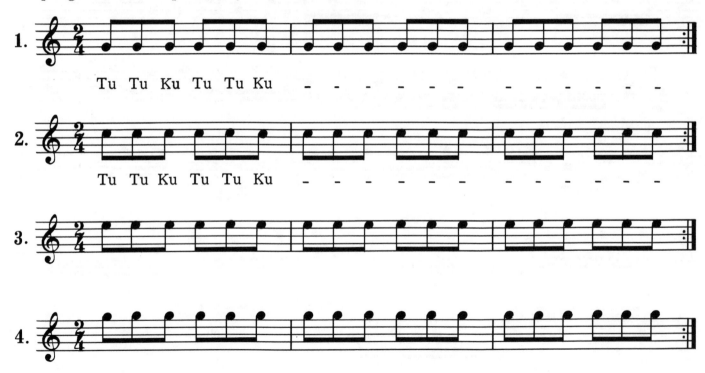

5.

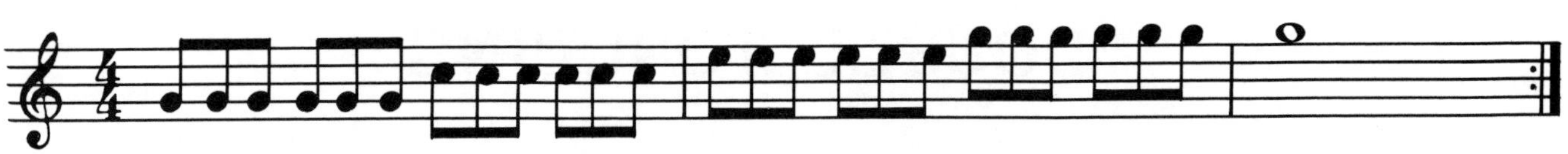

6.

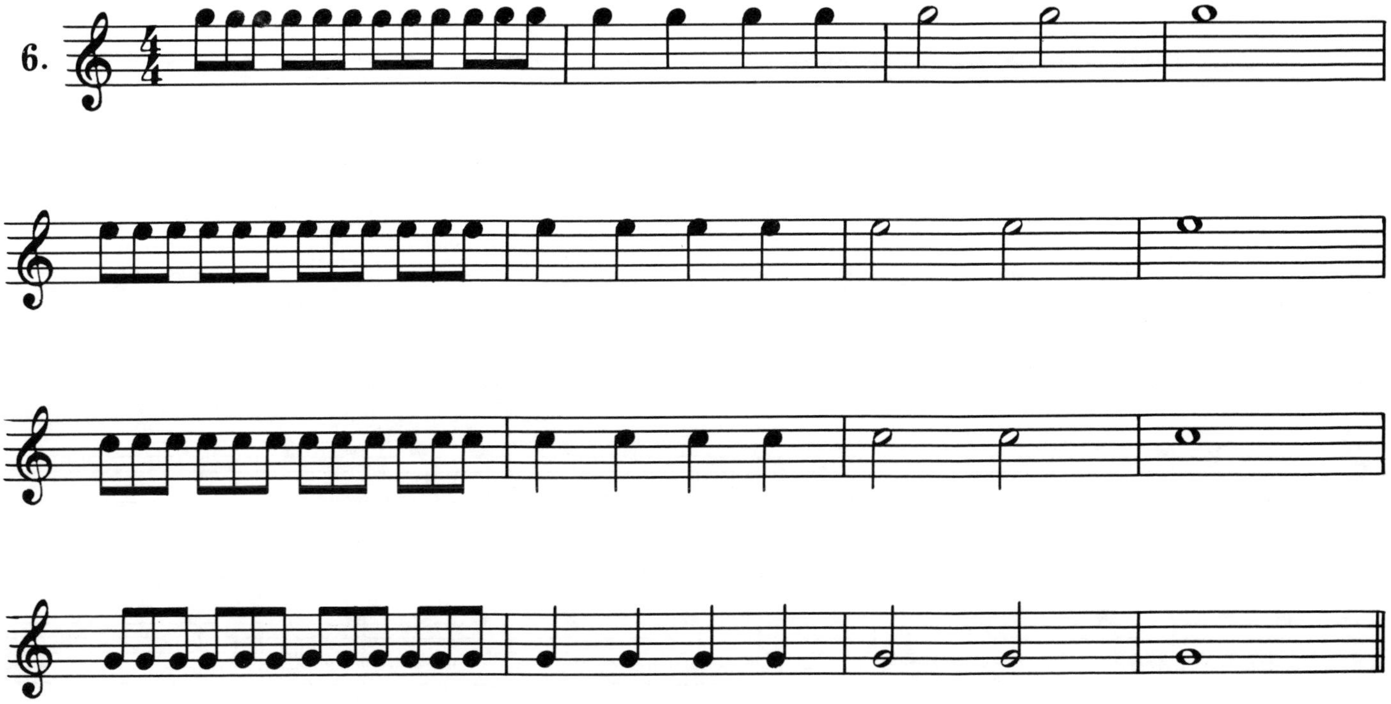

DOUBLE TONGUING

Double tonguing may be taken up after one can play triple tonguing evenly and at a moderate speed.

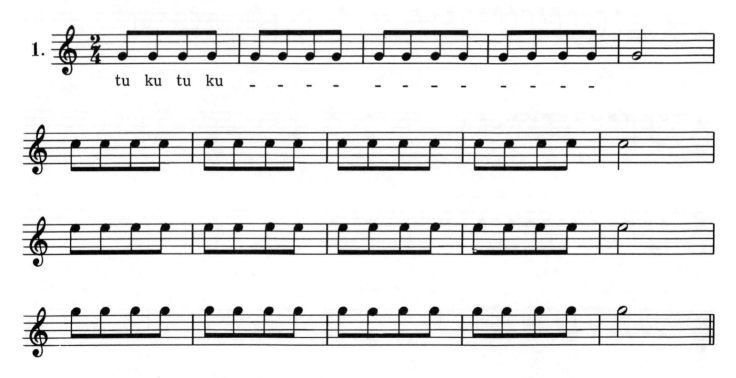

Hold for three beats.

2. tu tu ku tu

ASSEMBLY

DRILL

TO THE COLORS

RECALL

Moderately

TATTOO

Fast

TAPS

FIRST CALL

REVEILLE

MESS CALL

Moderate

MEMORIES

Slowly

GOOD FRIENDS

THE RAINBOW

HARVEST TIME

YOU'RE IN THE ARMY NOW

OLD SOLDIERS

Moderate

OVER THE TOP

HIT THE TRAIL

PLEASANT DREAMS

BUGLER'S PARADE

Brisk march tempo

CLOUDS ADRIFTING

FOREST CAPERS

TWILIGHT DREAMS

OLE BUDDIES

Slowly

LONESOME PINE

HAPPY DAYS

BRITISH BUGLE CALLS
REVEILLE

rall.

RETREAT

SOLO B♭ CORNET

TATTOO (LAST POST)

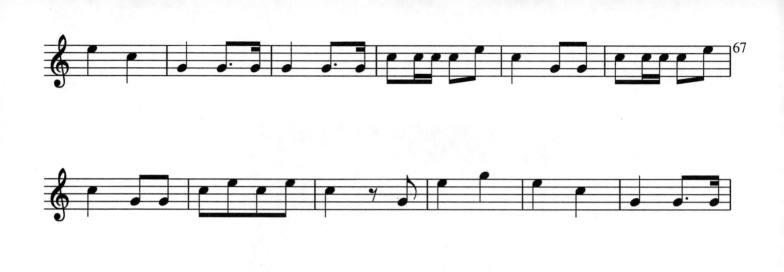

Great Music at Your Fingertips